# Bony Puzzle

by Lisa **Thompson**
illustrated by Lisa **Thompson**
and **Matthew Stapleton**

**PICTURE WINDOW BOOKS**
Minneapolis, Minnesota

Editor: Jacqueline A. Wolfe
Managing Editor: Catherine Neitge
Story Consultant: Terry Flaherty
Page Production: Melissa Kes
Creative Director: Keith Griffin
Editorial Director: Carol Jones

First American edition published in 2006 by
Picture Window Books
5115 Excelsior Boulevard
Suite 232
Minneapolis, MN 55416
1-877-845-8392
www.picturewindowbooks.com

First published in Australia in 2004 by
Blake Publishing Pty Ltd
ABN 50 074 266 023
108 Main Rd
Clayton South VIC 3168

© Blake Publishing Pty Ltd Australia 2004

Printed in the United States of America.

Library of Congress Cataloging-in-Publication Data

Thompson, Lisa, 1969-
Bony puzzle / by Lisa Thompson ; illustrated by Lisa Thompson and Matthew Stapleton.— 1st
American ed.
p. cm. — (Read-it! chapter books) (Wonder wits)
Summary: When Luke and Sophie go in search of people who figure out what dinosaurs
looked like and how they lived, they discover piecing together an accurate model of a dinosaur
includes science, art, imagination, and endless questioning.
ISBN 1-4048-1345-4 (hardcover)
[1. Dinosaurs—Fiction. 2. Paleontologists—Fiction.] I. Stapleton, Matthew, ill. II. Title. III. Series.
PZ7.T371634Bon 2005
[Fic]—dc22
2005009824

# Table of Contents

## More Stuff

"Careful! Remember, what's inside is very fragile," said Mr. Costa, as Luke and Sophie gently placed another box inside his new shed.

When it was safely on the floor, Mr. Costa said, "Just one more box to move and the job's done—bet that will make you smile!"

But Luke and his best friend, Sophie, didn't feel like smiling.

Luke and Sophie didn't

They liked helping Sophie's neighbor, Mr. Costa, but today they had other things on their minds.

Mr. Costa had never seen Sophie and Luke like this. All morning, he'd tried to make them forget their troubles. But nothing had worked, not even his penguin-shuffle dance.

"OK, you two," said Mr. Costa, "what's going on?"

"Not what—who," said Luke.

"Nicolas Wilson," added Sophie.

"World's biggest cheater," Luke added.

There was a whistle from the bottom of Mr. Costa's driveway. Luke and Sophie peeked out of the shed.

"Oh no, it's him," sighed Sophie. She stepped outside, followed by Luke. Mr. Costa watched through the window.

"What do you want, Wilson?" asked Luke. "Nothing to cheat on around here."

Nicolas ignored Luke and strolled up the driveway carrying his skateboard. "Your mom said I'd find you here," he said to Sophie.

Oh no ... here comes

"I wanted to stop by and tell you not to waste your time," Nicolas said.

"What are you talking about?" demanded Sophie.

"The Clever Creators' Competition." He smiled. "I'm going to win first place with the mini-rocket launch I'm organizing. So you shouldn't bother entering."

"You're organizing?" cried Sophie. "You can't organize your brain to switch on in the morning! How can you organize a rocket launch, let alone build one?"

Nicolas Wilson.

On/Off

"Yeah! Who's doing your work this time, Wilson?" Luke asked. "Is your dad paying someone to make it and then teach you how to work it? If that's the case, they'd better make it really, really simple."

Nicolas looked stunned, but he recovered. "Ahh, don't be sore losers. Do yourselves a favor and leave the competition to those who know what they're doing." He smirked and winked at Sophie.

"Quit it!" she yelled.

Winners are

"I can't help it," said Nicolas, breaking into a cheesy smile. "Winners are grinners, you know." He stepped onto his skateboard. "Too bad you two will never know the feeling," he called as he rode away.

"He's got to be the most annoying, cheating rat I've ever known," Sophie said through clenched teeth. "Ohhhh, I wish he'd get caught once—just once! He never does his own work. It's so unfair!"

Luke's face burned.

"So that's Nicolas Wilson," said Mr. Costa, coming out of the shed. "What is this Clever Creators' Competition?"

"It's a contest for Science Week," said Luke. "We're supposed to design an exhibit."

"If you win, your exhibit becomes part of the Science Museum," added Sophie.

"What are you two doing?" asked Mr. Costa.

The Clever Creators'

"Nothing," mumbled Luke. "What's the point? Wilson's already got first place. I can't see anything beating his rocket launch idea."

"What?" cried Mr. Costa. "Nicolas only came over because he knows you will do a better exhibit than him, even if he hires someone to do it for him! He's just trying to scare you so you won't enter."

Competition is on!

"I can think of one subject that always captures people's imaginations," said Mr. Costa. "But people rarely know about the creators behind the creations. It would make a fantastic exhibit. And you've been helping to move parts of it all morning."

"What?" asked Luke.

Mr. Costa opened the lid of the last box they had moved. He carefully unwrapped one of the objects.

Some scientists believe less than 10% of dinosaur

"Rocks? What's so special about rocks?"
asked Luke.

"Not rocks, Luke. They're fossils," said Sophie.

"Dinosaur fossils actually," said Mr. Costa. "This is a
tooth from a dinosaur." He unwrapped another fossil.
"And this is a dinosaur's footprint."

"Where did you get them?" asked Sophie, amazed.

"Oh, searching for dinosaur fossils is a hobby of mine. Haven't you ever wondered about the clever people who work out what dinosaurs looked like, using clues like this?" Mr. Costa pointed to a tooth.

"Bit by bit, they piece together an animal that disappeared 65 million years ago. Then they make images and models so we all know what they looked like."

Have you ever wondered about the peopl

"Dinosaur creators!" exclaimed Sophie. "What an excellent idea! We'll do an exhibit on dinosaur creators. What do you think, Luke?"

"It's perfect," he said.

"Well," said Mr. Costa, "let me show you pictures of the first dinosaur models and the people who made them."

New Years Eve 185

Mr. Costa showed Luke and Sophie a picture of a group of people eating dinner inside a dinosaur. Sophie read aloud the caption below the picture, "New Years Eve 1853."

"What an excellent idea, to throw a party inside a dinosaur!" said Luke.

A party was held inside one of the

"This was one of the first models of a dinosaur ever made," explained Mr. Costa.

"What kind of dinosaur is it?" asked Luke.

"An *Iguanodon*," said Mr. Costa. "These people were leading scientists of the day. They were invited to see the first life-size model of a dinosaur by the two people who created it. Richard Owen was a scientist, and Waterhouse Hawkins was a sculptor."

**Iguana**

**Bird**

"Before this model, people weren't sure what these creatures looked like," said Mr. Costa. "In fact, it was Richard Owen who came up with the name *Dinosauria*. It means 'fearfully great lizard' in Greek."

"How did they figure out what dinosaurs looked like?" asked Luke.

"Well, Richard Owen was a professor of anatomy. He studied the structure of different animals, compared their skeletons, and saw what they had in common," said Mr. Costa.

*Dinosauria means "fearfully*

**The *Iguanodon* did not have
the lizardlike hips of an iguana.
Instead, it had birdlike hips.**

"Richard Owen used his knowledge of anatomy
when looking at groups of dinosaur fossils."

"What did he see?" asked Sophie, intrigued.

"He realized dinosaurs had legs directly under
their bodies. They weren't like the legs we see on
lizards today."

"How did this help Richard Owen make a
skeleton? He didn't have all the bones," said Luke.

great lizard" in Greek.

**Birdlike beak**

**Speed of an ostrich**

**Lizardlike skin**

"Well, he compared extinct dinosaurs with animals of his time. He used his knowledge of how animals' bodies are put together to fill in the blanks. He once predicted the structure of an entire bird by studying just one bone fragment!" exclaimed Mr. Costa.

"How clever!" said Sophie.

"Yes, it was clever, but he also made mistakes," said Mr. Costa.

Bit by bit, a picture of what

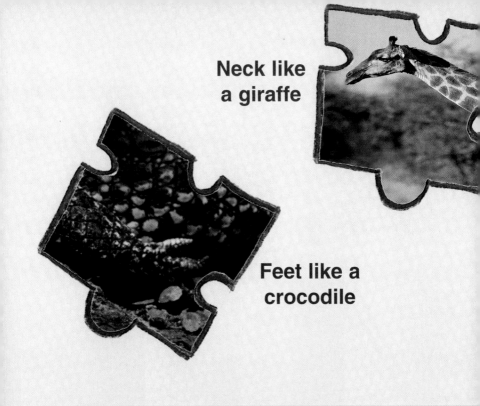

**Neck like a giraffe**

**Feet like a crocodile**

"There was still a lot of guesswork involved. People were just starting to find fossils. They didn't have the amount of information we have today. The puzzle of what these creatures looked like and how they lived was just starting to emerge. For instance, the *Iguanodon* in the picture has a spike on its head. We now know that this is wrong. The *Iguanodon* had two spiked thumbs."

a dinosaur looked like emerged.

"How did the sculptor, Waterhouse Hawkins, make the giant model of the dinosaur?" asked Luke.

"First, Waterhouse Hawkins did lots of drawings based on Richard Owen's ideas. Then he made small models to make sure the proportions were correct. Finally, he made giant structures out of concrete and iron. No one had ever seen anything like it. These two men were the pioneers of dinosaur modeling."

Paleo means "ancient" or "from the past

"Who does it today, Mr. Costa?" asked Luke.

"I have a friend, Erica Monroe, who can answer questions about that. She is a paleontologist," Mr. Costa said.

"A pale … what?" asked Luke.

"An expert who studies fossils," said Mr. Costa. "I want Erica to look at these recent finds, so I'll give her a call. You two should visit her tomorrow. We can't have Nicolas Wilson, or his helpers, getting too much of a head start!"

Paleontology is the study of the past.

Erica Monroe strode across the lobby of the museum to greet them.

"Hi, Luke and Sophie, I'm Erica," she said, smiling. "Mr. Costa told me about your competition. He also said you would be bringing something to show me."

"Here they are," Sophie said as she handed over Mr. Costa's fossils, wrapped in special packaging.

Luke took a book from his backpack, saying, "He also said you would need this."

Fossils are formed in rocks from

"Ah! His field notebook. Yes, that will be very handy," Erica said, paging through it.

"What's in it?" asked Sophie.

"Lots of important information," Erica said, "such as the place and the exact rock layer where the fossils were found. This helps us determine roughly when the dinosaur died and even the kind of environment it lived in. So let's take these down to the lab."

mud and sand left by water or wind.

"Can we take pictures for our competition?" asked Sophie.

"Of course," said Erica. "Actually you've come at a good time. We've just received a container of fossils from a dig site."

Luke and Sophie followed Erica down a long hallway. She led them into a room where scientists and lab workers were unpacking and carefully cleaning the fossils. They took photos as bones were strengthened and repaired with special glue.

Special glues and plastics make sure

Other technicians then took molds of the fossils. That way, Erica explained, scientists would study the copies and not need to handle the precious fossils.

Luke picked up a copy of a dinosaur's skull. "Wow, this looks like the real thing!"

"That's the idea," said Erica. "Follow me, and I'll show you what I think is the most exciting place of all—the identifying room."

he fossil will be preserved forever.

Erica led them into a room where people worked at computers. She passed Mr. Costa's fossils to an assistant, saying, "We'll check our fossil database to see if there have been similar teeth and footprints discovered already. Did you know that the remains of over 800 different types of dinosaurs have been found already? But we think there might be thousands of different species! So there are plenty more waiting to be discovered."

The long process of

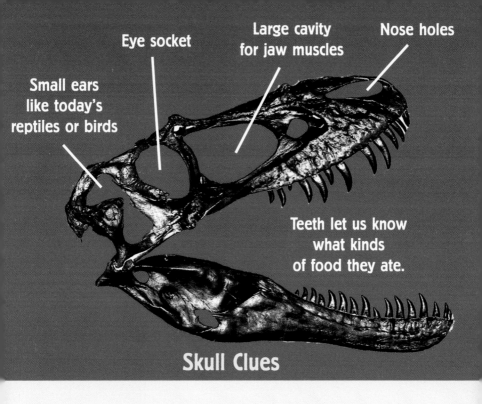

Small ears
like today's
reptiles or birds

Eye socket

Large cavity
for jaw muscles

Nose holes

Teeth let us know
what kinds
of food they ate.

**Skull Clues**

"What happens after they are identified?"
asked Luke.

"The long process of studying the clues held by
each fossil begins. Take a look at this skull." Erica
pointed to the many holes. "From the holes, we
can tell the size of the eyes, ears, nasal passages,
and brain. This helps give us an image of how the
dinosaur could see, hear, smell, and think—even
the kinds of sounds it made."

Erica picked up what looked like a leg bone and said, "Dinosaurs are quite unlike anything on Earth today, so we must always look closely at the bones they have left behind. We look for grooves, scars, and bumps on the bone to show us where muscles were attached. These help us figure out the shape and size of the animal."

Bone grooves, scars, and bumps give

"Do you look at animals that are around today and compare them with dinosaurs?" asked Sophie.

"Sure!" said Erica. "We study animals that we know have similarities to the dinosaur, such as birds like the emu and reptiles like the crocodile. They give us ideas about what dinosaurs looked like and how they moved."

Erica headed toward another room and said, "Now I'll show you how technology helps us refine our theories."

lues to the dinosaur's size and shape.

"Let me introduce my top dinosaur designer, Ben," said Erica. "Ben helps us bring dinosaurs to life so we can test our theories."

A dinosaur with two long legs and a large beak was on Ben's computer screen. Its walk was being compared to an emu's.

"With computers, we can study dinosaur skeletons more closely and make detailed and accurate comparisons," explained Ben.

For a long time, people thought dinosaurs

"The legs of some dinosaurs appear to have similar bone structures to modern, flightless birds, like the ostrich and the emu. So I am exploring whether these dinosaurs moved like these birds. For a long time, people thought all dinosaurs were slow-moving creatures, but that may be wrong," said Ben.

Erica showed them how to work out the dinosaur's range of movement on the computer. Luke used a program to work out the running speed of the dinosaur.

were slow-moving, but were they?

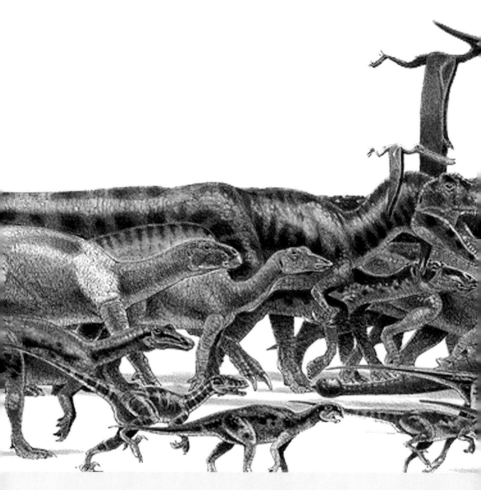

Sophie adjusted the tail and head of the dinosaur as it moved, and then froze it in different positions.

"This is important when we build our life-sized models. We want to pose them in natural positions," said Ben.

Next, Ben showed them how to re-create noises a *T. rex* might make, based on noises made by a crocodile.

Sophie and Luke played around with the color of the dinosaur.

The fastest dinosaur was the Struthiomimus. It could reach speed

"We don't have much evidence for the colors of dinosaurs," explained Ben. "We have found fossils of scales and skin and even feathers. But we still look at the skin colors of animals today and make a guesstimate."

"What's a guesstimate?" asked Sophie.

"It's a bit of a guess and a bit of an estimate based on the evidence we have found so far," said Erica. "We also use guesstimates when figuring out how much a dinosaur weighed."

of 40 mph (64km/hr). An ostrich can reach 50 mph (80 km/hr).

Erica's assistant came into the room. She read a result for one of Mr. Costa's fossils outloud, "It seems that we have a tooth of a *Stegosaur*, but we don't have a result for the footprint yet."

"You mean Mr. Costa might have discovered a whole new species?" asked Sophie excitedly.

"If he has, we should name it a Costasaurus!" Luke said.

What's in a name? *Struthio* is Latin for "ostrich."

"We'll have to find some more evidence first," smiled Ben, "but it's possible!"

"I'm afraid I have to go," said Erica. "Feel free to look around. Don't be afraid to ask questions. A questioning mind is an important tool used to find out what dinosaurs were really like. Remember, if questions weren't asked, we would still think *Iguanodons* had spikes on their heads. Good luck!"

Struthiomimus means "ostrich mimic."

# Chapter 5
## Winners are Grinners

The countdown to Nicolas Wilson's mini-rocket launch began.

10 … 9 … 8 … 7 …

A large crowd gathered. The judges of the competition sat in the front row. Luke, Sophie, and Mr. Costa watched from the side. Luke could see Nicolas grin as his hand hovered over the launch button.

6 … 5 … 4 … 3 … 2 … 1 …

Nicolas hit the button and yelled, "Blast off!"

Nothing happened.

The rocket sat on its launch pad. Nicolas pressed the button again and again.

Still nothing happened.

Nicolas looked horrified. He wiggled the controls. "Just a small problem with the ... um, circuit board." He looked very pale as he pretended to do some repairs. "I may need to call someone to help me fix it," he mumbled.

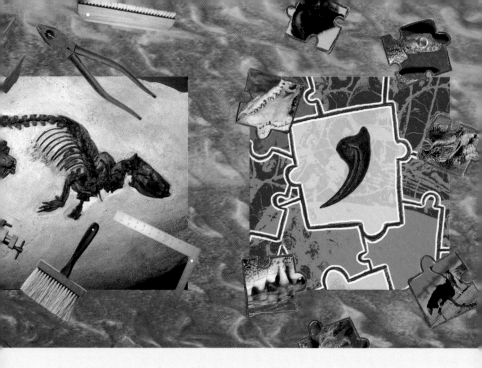

"No need!" said the head judge. "You can talk me through how it is meant to work and I'll judge you on that. The other judges can move on to the dinosaur exhibit."

Nicolas had no color left in his face. "Talk you through it?" he whimpered. "Me? Now?"

The other judges and the crowd moved toward Luke and Sophie's exhibit.

"We present the Dinosaur Creators!" cried Sophie, as Luke opened the curtain. The crowd gasped and burst into applause.

Discovery of fossil ... cleaning ...

Sophie and Luke had created their exhibit inside a model of an *Iguanodon*. On this *Iguanodon*, however, there was a spike on each thumb and not on its head!

Inside the dinosaur were cross-sections, photos, and models. They showed the procedure that palaeontologists, scientists, lab workers, and designers follow when making a dinosaur model. There is the discovery of a dinosaur fossil, followed by cleaning, restoring, molding, identifying, and comparing. Finally, a computer image is produced and a life-size model is created.

Every part of the exhibit had been created by Luke and Sophie, except for the still unidentified dinosaur footprint in the plastic case—which Mr. Costa was happily guarding.

The judges were very impressed. Luke and Sophie overheard their comments.

"It's exceptional."

"It is a sure fire winner!"

Sophie and Luke were thrilled that everyone appreciated their hard work.

Dinosaur grins are

Sophie looked around for Nicolas, but he was gone. "Don't tell me he never even saur-us," she giggled.

"I'm sure Nicolas can catch our exhibit at the Science Museum when it's there." Luke looked at the growing crowd. "It looks like it will be there for a long time."

Nicolas was right about one thing, thought Luke, smiling. Winners are grinners. At that very moment, Luke guesstimated his smile was as big as any *T. rex's*!

the biggest of all!

# Dinosaur

The *Iguanodon* got its name because its teeth looked like giant versions of the living iguana from the Galapagos Islands.

When Gideon Mantell first found the teeth of the Iguanodon in 1822, other scientists believed they were from a rhinoceros.

# Facts

For hundreds of years, the Blackfoot Indians of Canada thought that the dinosaur bones they found were from their ancestors.

In China, doctors have been collecting dinosaur teeth for over 2,000 years. They believed they came from dragons.

One dinosaur bone was thought to belong to a giant race of man that is now extinct!

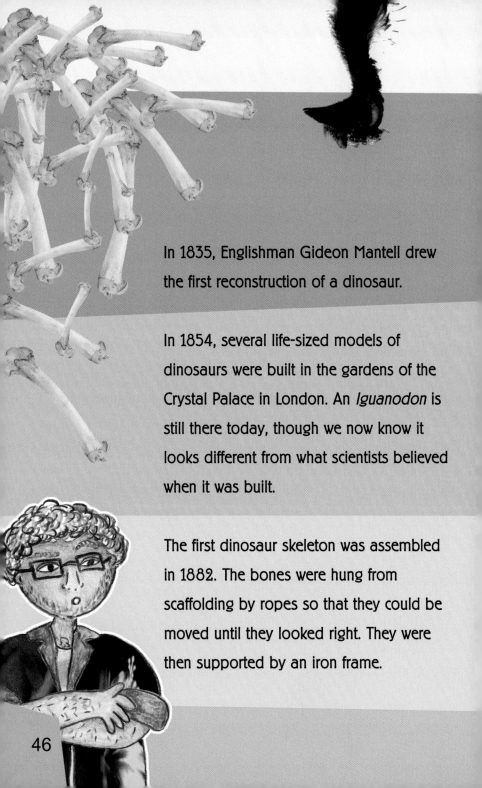

In 1835, Englishman Gideon Mantell drew the first reconstruction of a dinosaur.

In 1854, several life-sized models of dinosaurs were built in the gardens of the Crystal Palace in London. An *Iguanodon* is still there today, though we now know it looks different from what scientists believed when it was built.

The first dinosaur skeleton was assembled in 1882. The bones were hung from scaffolding by ropes so that they could be moved until they looked right. They were then supported by an iron frame.

Fossils of dinosaur droppings have helped scientists discover what dinosaurs ate.

Fossil footprints give clues about the foot shape as well as the weight and speed of the dinosaur.

The *Eoraptor* is thought to be the earliest type of dinosaur found. It lived 228 million years ago and was barely as tall as a German shepherd dog.

There may be more dinosaurs than scientists know about. But we will never know for sure because their fossils have not been found.

Read all about Luke and Sophie's unusual adventures in these great books!

1. Artrageous
2. Wonder Worlds
3. Wild Ideas
4. Look Out!
5. What's Next?
6. Game Plan
7. Gadget Hero
8. Bony Puzzle

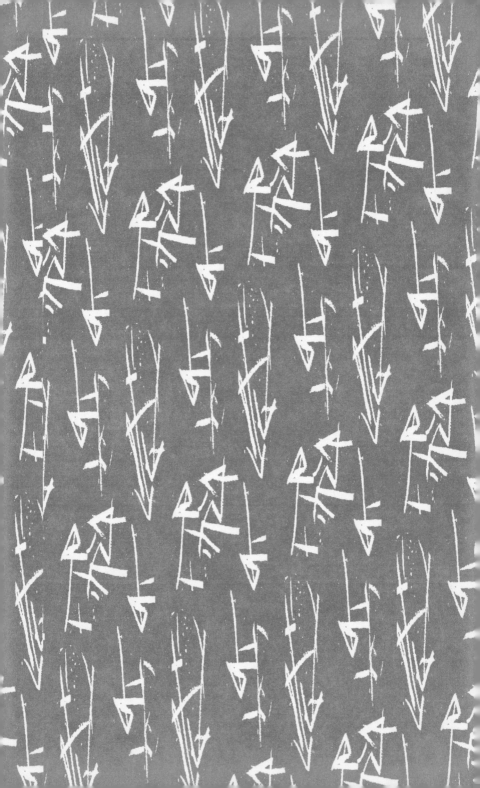